SNIP
SNAP

BEN NEWMAN

The crab goes…

...SNIP, SNIP!

The water goes
SPLOSH, SPLOSH!

The crocodile goes

...SNAP!

The fish go
SPLISH, SPLASH!

The bird goes
FLAP, FLAP!

The branch goes
CREAK, CREAK!

...WOBBLE!

The egg goes
BOING...

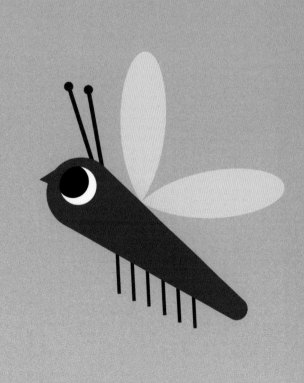

The eggs go CRICK!

CRACK!

The lobster goes...

Inspired by my son, Wilbur Newman
and my friend, Alexis Deacon – B.N.

First published 2021 by Macmillan Children's Books
an imprint of Pan Macmillan
The Smithson,
6 Briset Street,
London EC1M 5NR
Associated companies throughout the world

www.panmacmillan.com

ISBN: 978-1-5290-5145-2

Illustrations and text copyright © Ben Newman 2021

The right of Ben Newman to be identified as the author and illustrator of this work has been
asserted by him in accordance with the Copyright, Designs and Patents Act 1988.

1 3 5 7 9 8 6 4 2

A CIP catalogue record for this book is available from
the British Library.

Printed in China